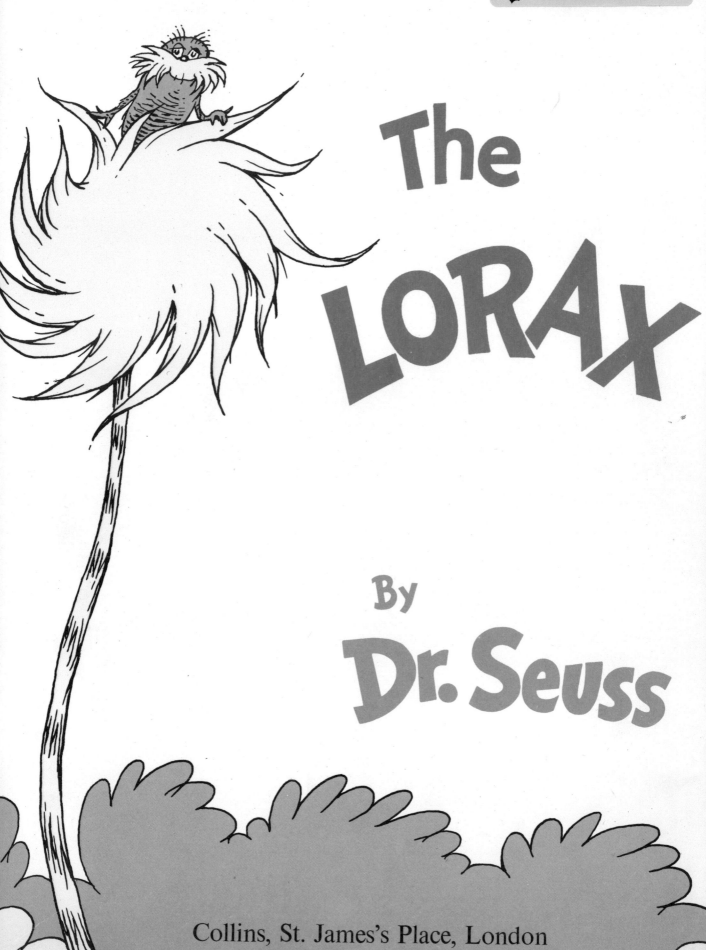

The LORAX

By Dr. Seuss

Collins, St. James's Place, London

For Audrey, Lark and Lea

With Love

FIRST PUBLISHED IN GREAT BRITAIN 1972
COPYRIGHT © 1971 BY DR. SEUSS AND A. S. GEISEL
ISBN 0 00 195458 X
MADE AND PRINTED IN GREAT BRITAIN BY
WM COLLINS SONS & CO LTD GLASGOW

At the far end of town
where the Grickle-grass grows
and the wind smells slow-and-sour when it blows
and no birds ever sing excepting old crows...
is the Street of the Lifted Lorax.

And deep in the Grickle-grass, some people say,
if you look deep enough you can still see, today,
where the Lorax once stood
just as long as it could
before somebody lifted the Lorax away.

What *was* the Lorax?
And why was it there?
And why was it lifted and taken somewhere
from the far end of town where the Grickle-grass grows?
The old Once-ler still lives here.
Ask him. *He* knows.

You won't see the Once-ler.
Don't knock at his door.
He stays in his Lerkim on top of his store.
He lurks in his Lerkim, cold under the roof,
where he makes his own clothes
out of miff-muffered moof.
And on special dank midnights in August,
he peeks
out of the shutters
and sometimes he speaks
and tells how the Lorax was lifted away.

He'll tell you, perhaps...
if you're willing to pay.

On the end of a rope
he lets down a tin pail
and you have to toss in fifteen pence
and a nail
and the shell of a great-great-great-
grandfather snail.

Then he pulls up the pail,
makes a most careful count
to see if you've paid him
the proper amount.

Then he hides what you paid him
away in his Snuvv,
his secret strange hole
in his gruvvulous glove.

Then he grunts, "I will call you by Whisper-ma-Phone,
for the secrets I tell are for your ears alone."

SLUPP!
Down slupps the Whisper-ma-Phone to your ear
and the old Once-ler's whispers are not very clear,
since they have to come down
through a snergelly hose,
and he sounds
as if he had
smallish bees up his nose.

"Now I'll tell you," he says, with his teeth sounding grey
"how the Lorax got lifted and taken away...

    It all started way back...
    such a long, long time back...

Way back in the days when the grass was still green
and the pond was still wet
and the clouds were still clean,
and the song of the Swomee-Swans rang out in space...
one morning, I came to this glorious place.
And I first saw the trees!
The Truffula Trees!
The bright-coloured tufts of the Truffula Trees!
Mile after mile in the fresh morning breeze.

And, under the trees, I saw Brown Bar-ba-loots
frisking about in their Bar-ba-loot suits
as they played in the shade and ate Truffula Fruits.

From the rippulous pond
came the comfortable sound
of the Humming-Fish humming
while splashing around.

But those *trees!* Those *trees!*
Those Truffula Trees!
All my life I'd been searching
for trees such as these.
The touch of their tufts
was much softer than silk.
And they had the sweet smell
of fresh butterfly milk.

I felt a great leaping
of joy in my heart.
I knew just what I'd do!
I unloaded my cart.

In no time at all, I had built a small shop.
Then I chopped down a Truffula Tree with one chop.
And with great skilful skill and with great speedy speed,
I took the soft tuft. And I knitted a Thneed!

The instant I'd finished, I heard a *ga-Zump!*
I looked.
I saw something pop out of the stump
of the tree I'd chopped down. It was sort of a man.
Describe him?...That's hard. I don't know if I can.

He was shortish. And oldish.
And brownish. And mossy.
And he spoke with a voice
that was sharpish and bossy.

"Mister!" he said with a sawdusty sneeze,
"I am the Lorax. I speak for the trees.
I speak for the trees, for the trees have no tongues.
And I'm asking you, sir, at the top of my lungs"—
he was very upset as he shouted and puffed—
"What's that THING you've made out of my Truffula tuft?"

"Look, Lorax," I said. "There's no cause for alarm.
I chopped just one tree. I am doing no harm.
I'm being quite useful. This thing is a Thneed.
A Thneed's a Fine-Something-That-All-People-Need!
It's a shirt. It's a sock. It's a glove. It's a hat.
But it has *other* uses. Yes, far beyond that.
You can use it for carpets. For pillows! For sheets!
Or curtains! Or covers for bicycle seats!"

The Lorax said,
"Sir! You are crazy with greed.
There is no one on earth
who would buy that fool Thneed!"

But the very next minute I proved he was wrong.
For, just at that minute, a chap came along,
and he thought that the Thneed I had knitted was great.
He happily bought it for three ninety-eight.

I laughed at the Lorax, "You poor stupid guy!
You never can tell what some people will buy."

"I repeat," cried the Lorax,
"I speak for the trees!"

"I'm busy," I told him.
"Shut up, if you please."

I rushed 'cross the room, and in no time at all,
built a radio-phone. I put in a quick call.
I called all my brothers and uncles and aunts
and I said, "Listen here! Here's a wonderful chance
for the whole Once-ler Family to get mighty rich!
Get over here fast! Take the road to North Nitch.
Turn left at Weehawken. Sharp right at South Stitch."

And, in no time at all,
in the factory I built,
the whole Once-ler Family
was working full tilt.
We were all knitting Thneeds
just as busy as bees,
to the sound of the chopping
of Truffula Trees.

Then...
Oh! Baby! Oh!
How my business did grow!
Now, chopping one tree
at a time
was too slow.

So I quickly invented my Super-Axe-Hacker
which whacked off four Truffula Trees at one smacker.
We were making Thneeds
four times as fast as before!
And that Lorax?...
He didn't show up any more.

But the next week
he knocked
on my new office door.

He snapped, "I'm the Lorax who speaks for the trees
which you seem to be chopping as fast as you please.
But I'm *also* in charge of the Brown Bar-ba-loots
who played in the shade in their Bar-ba-loot suits
and happily lived, eating Truffula Fruits.

"NOW...thanks to your hacking my trees to the ground,
there's not enough Truffula Fruit to go 'round.
And my poor Bar-ba-loots are all getting the crummies
because they have gas, and no food, in their tummies!

"They loved living here. But I can't let them stay.
They'll have to find food. And I hope that they may.
Good luck, boys," he cried. And he sent them away.

I, the Once-ler, felt sad
as I watched them all go.
BUT...
business is business!
And business must grow
regardless of crummies in tummies, you know.

I meant no harm. I most truly did not.
But I had to grow bigger. So bigger I got.
I biggered my factory. I biggered my roads.
I biggered my wagons. I biggered the loads
of the Thneeds I shipped out. I was shipping them forth
to the South! To the East! To the West! To the North!
I went right on biggering...selling more Thneeds.
And I biggered my money, which everyone needs.

YOU NEED
THNEED

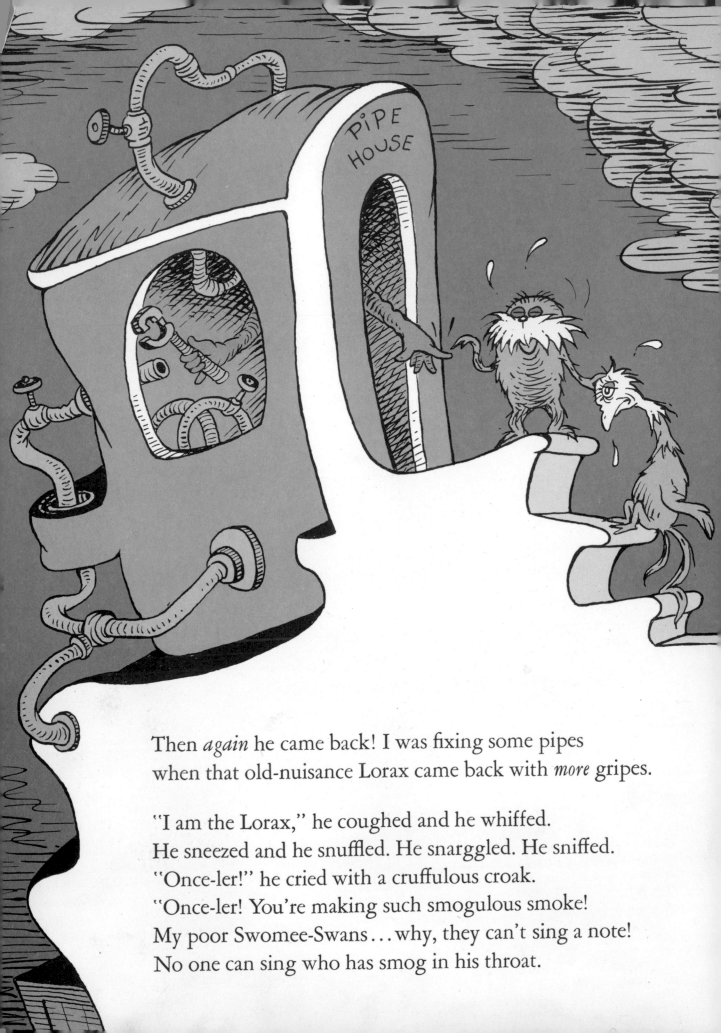

Then *again* he came back! I was fixing some pipes
when that old-nuisance Lorax came back with *more* gripes.

"I am the Lorax," he coughed and he whiffed.
He sneezed and he snuffled. He snarggled. He sniffed.
"Once-ler!" he cried with a cruffulous croak.
"Once-ler! You're making such smogulous smoke!
My poor Swomee-Swans ... why, they can't sing a note!
No one can sing who has smog in his throat.

"And so," said the Lorax,
"—please pardon my cough—
they cannot live here.
So I'm sending them off.

"Where will they go?...
I don't hopefully know.

They may have to fly for a month...or a year...
To escape from the smog you've smogged-up around here.

"What's *more*," snapped the Lorax. (His dander was up.)
"Let me say a few words about Gluppity-Glupp.
Your machinery chugs on, day and night without stop
making Gluppity-Glupp. Also Schloppity-Schlopp.
And what do you do with this leftover goo?...
I'll show you. You dirty old Once-ler man, you!

"You're glumping the pond where the Humming-Fish hummed!
No more can they hum, for their gills are all gummed.
So I'm sending them off. Oh, their future is dreary.
They'll walk on their fins and get woefully weary
in search of some water that isn't so smeary.
I hear things are just as bad up in Lake Erie."

And then I got mad.
I got terribly mad.
I yelled at the Lorax, "Now listen here, Dad!
All you do is yap-yap and say, 'Bad! Bad! Bad! Bad!'
Well, I have my rights, sir, and I'm telling *you*
I intend to go on doing just what I do!
And, for your information, you Lorax, I'm figgering
on biggering

and BIGGERING

and **BIGGERING**

and **BIGGERING**,

turning MORE Truffula Trees into Thneeds
which everyone, EVERYONE, *EVERYONE* needs!"

And at that very moment, we heard a loud whack!
From outside in the fields came a sickening smack
of an axe on a tree. Then we heard the tree fall.
The very last Truffula Tree of them all!

No more trees. No more Thneeds. No more work to be done.
So, in no time, my uncles and aunts, every one,
all waved me good-bye. They jumped into my cars
and drove away under the smoke-smuggered stars.

Now all that was left 'neath the bad-smelling sky
was my big empty factory...
the Lorax...
and I.

The Lorax said nothing. Just gave me a glance...
just gave me a very sad, sad backward glance...
as he lifted himself by the seat of his pants.
And I'll never forget the grim look on his face
when he heisted himself and took leave of this place,
through a hole in the smog, without leaving a trace.

And all that the Lorax left here in this mess
was a small pile of rocks, with the one word . . .
"UNLESS."
Whatever *that* meant, well, I just couldn't guess.

That was long, long ago.
But each day since that day
I've sat here and worried
and worried away.
Through the years, while my buildings
have fallen apart,
I've worried about it
with all of my heart.

"But *now*," says the Once-ler,
"Now that *you're* here,
the word of the Lorax seems perfectly clear.
UNLESS someone like you
cares a whole awful lot,
nothing is going to get better.
It's not.

"SO...
Catch!" calls the Once-ler.
He lets something fall.
"It's a Truffula Seed.
It's the last one of all!
You're in charge of the last of the Truffula Seeds.
And Truffula Trees are what everyone needs.
Plant a new Truffula. Treat it with care.
Give it clean water. And feed it fresh air.
Grow a forest. Protect it from axes that hack.
Then the Lorax
and all of his friends
may come back."

Can I Play FARMER, FARMER

Jill Paton Walsh
Illustrated by Jolyne Knox

THE BODLEY HEAD
LONDON

Rachel and her friends were playing Farmer, Farmer. The teacher had let them out of school a few minutes early, because it was such a fine day, and they were playing until their mothers came to meet them at the school gate. First, they chose a Farmer. Rachel counted round them with a dipping rhyme.

'Inky, pinky, ponky,
Daddy bought a donkey,
The donkey died, and Daddy
cried,
Inky, pinky, ponky,
You – are – IT!'

When she got to 'IT!' she was pointing at Alice, so Alice was the Farmer.

Alice stood in the middle of the playground, and everyone else lined up against the playground wall.

They said: 'Farmer, Farmer, can we cross your golden river?'

'No!' shouted Alice, being the Farmer. 'The water is too deep!'

The children asked again. 'Farmer, Farmer, can we cross your golden river?'

'No!' shouted the Farmer. 'The corn is being reaped!'

But the third time, when everyone shouted, 'Farmer, Farmer, can we cross your golden river?', Alice said 'you can't cross my river unless you have *blue*!'

Lucy had a blue T-shirt. She
walked quietly across to the
other side of the playground.
Barbara had blue socks.
Gemma had blue hair-grip.
They could cross safely too.

Rachel had to run and run with the Farmer chasing her, because she wasn't wearing anything blue. She wasn't safe until she could touch the fence on the other side of the playground. If the Farmer caught you, you had to turn into one of his men, and help him catch other people.

In the next round the Farmer said, 'you can't cross my river unless you have yellow!'

Penny had yellow plastic sandals, and Gemma had a yellow sweater. They were all right. Rachel had to run again.

The third time Alice said, 'you can't cross my river unless you have white!' That wasn't clever of her; everybody had white vests and knickers. Everybody walked free.

The game went on and on until everybody had been caught. Rachel always got caught quite soon; she never seemed to have enough colours. Her mother liked clothes that matched.

By and by the mothers came to collect the children, and the game stopped. Rachel's big sister Alison was waiting for her at the gate. Alison came to fetch Rachel from school, and take her to their Gran's for tea, every Wednesday. 'Whatever were you running and shouting about, Rachel?' asked Alison.

'We were playing 'Farmer, Farmer,' said Rachel. 'It's my favourite game.'

'How do you play it?' asked Alison.

Rachel told her. 'I would have thought you would have played it too, Alison, when you were at my school, when you were little,' she said.

'We might have done,' said Alison. 'We played something called "Please Mr Crocodile" that sounds a bit like that. I can't really remember.'

Rachel was surprised. 'You can't remember!' she said. 'But what do you play at your new school?'

'We play tennis and netball, or we walk around and talk,' said Alison. 'We don't play baby games like yours.'

'But why not?' said Rachel.

'When you get more grown-up you think those games are boring,' said Alison. And here they were at Gran's house.

Gran had made tea for Rachel and Alison. She made them all their favourite things — hot buttered buns for Rachel, and bridge rolls with crab paste for Alison; a boiled egg with toast fingers to dip in it for Rachel, and flaky sausage rolls for Alison; chocolate cake all gooey in the middle for Rachel, and dark sticky gingerbread for Alison; fizzy lemonade for Rachel; and a pot of tea for Alison and for Gran herself.

After tea, Alison went upstairs to do her homework in Gran's spare bedroom, and Gran and Rachel sat together.

'I get fidgets in my fingers when I'm not knitting anything, Rachel,' said Gran. 'And I think I'll make a sweater for you, next. What colour would you like?'

'Could I have a blue one?' said Rachel.

'Yes,' said Gran.

'Could it have a bit of red in it?' asked Rachel.

'Yes,' said Gran.

'And a bit of yellow, and a bit of green?' said Rachel.

'Yes,' said Gran.

'And a bit of white, and a bit of black?' said Rachel.

'Yes,' said Gran. 'Are you sure you wouldn't like purple and pink?'

'I wouldn't like purple and pink instead,' said Rachel.

'Could I have them as well?'

'You'll look like a rainbow,' said Gran.

'Rainbows are nice,' said Rachel.

'All right,' said Gran. 'I'll use up lots of scraps of wool, and you shall have all the colours of the rainbow.'

'How many colours is that?' asked Rachel.

'Seven,' said Gran. 'Red, orange, yellow, green, blue, indigo, violet.'

'Tell me again,' said Rachel. 'I want to remember them.'

'Easy', said Gran. 'Richard of York gained battles in vain.'

'Pardon?' said Rachel.

'Richard for Red, Of for Orange, York for Yellow, Gained for Green, Battles for Blue, In for Indigo, Vain for Violet,' said Gran. 'Say it through and you've learned it all.'

'Richard of York gained battles in vain,' said Rachel. 'Red, orange, yellow, green, blue, indigo, violet . . . what about pink, Gran?'

'Pink is a shade of red,' said Gran.

'What about purple?' asked Rachel.

'Purple is another word for violet,' said Gran.

'But what about black and white, Gran?'

'Ah,' said Gran. 'Those are more difficult. The rainbows are made of light shining back at you from things. If no light at all shines back at you, you see black. So black isn't really a colour. And if all the colours in the light shine back at you at once you see white. So white is really all-coloured. There couldn't be black or white in a rainbow.'

'But in my sweater there could be. It could be better than a rainbow; it could have nine colours in it!'

'If you wanted them all, it could,' said Gran looking at Rachel with a rather surprised expression on her face.

'I do want them all,' Rachel said.

'Then help me go through my wool. We've got lots of colours to find for this rainbow special,' said Gran.

Gran was good at knitting; she was very quick. But when Rachel's mother saw the new sweater she was a little surprised.

'It's a bit gaudy,' she said. 'Gran usually has such good taste!'

'I like it,' said Rachel. 'Can I wear it to school?'

Next time everyone was playing Farmer, Farmer, Barbara was the Farmer. She said, 'you can't cross my river unless you have red!'

Rachel had red stripes in her sweater, so she walked proudly across.

Then Barbara said, 'you can't cross my river unless you have green!' Rachel walked across, with the others all running and screaming, and with Barbara chasing them like mad.

Then Barbara said 'You can't cross my river unless you have pink!' Rachel had pink. Rachel had red, orange, yellow, green, blue, indigo and violet. *And* Rachel had black. *And* Rachel had white. She kept just walking across the playground.

'This is a silly game!' she said. 'And I used to think it was lots of fun. Perhaps I'm getting grown-up like Alison.' Then she had another thought. She pulled Gran's sweater off, over her head, and hung it from the playground fence.

'Farmer, Farmer, can we cross your golden river?' she shouted, with all the others.

'You can't cross my river unless you have purple!' cried the Farmer.

All the purple Rachel had was in her sweater, hanging on the fence. She had to run and run.

'You can't cross my river unless you have orange!' said the Farmer. All the orange Rachel had was in her sweater, hanging on the fence. She had to run and run.

'You can't cross my river unless you have green!' called the Farmer. All the green that Rachel had was in her sweater, hanging on the fence, and she had to run with all the others.

'You can't cross my river unless you have blue!' said the Farmer. Rachel had to run again, and this time she got caught, and had to be one of the Farmer's men, and help him catch the others.

Only once, when the Farmer called for yellow, could Rachel walk proudly and safely across; she was wearing a pale yellow shirt and a bright yellow skirt. Her mother liked things to match.

And she changed her mind again. Farmer, Farmer was her favourite game of all! As for the nice new sweater, she could wear that to the park, and going to have tea with Gran, and to Gemma's birthday party, and going shopping on Saturday.

It would be cosy for coming to school on chilly mornings. It would cheer her up in reading lessons, and make sure the teacher saw her when she put up her hand in class to ask a question. But at playtime she would take it off, and hang it on the fence.

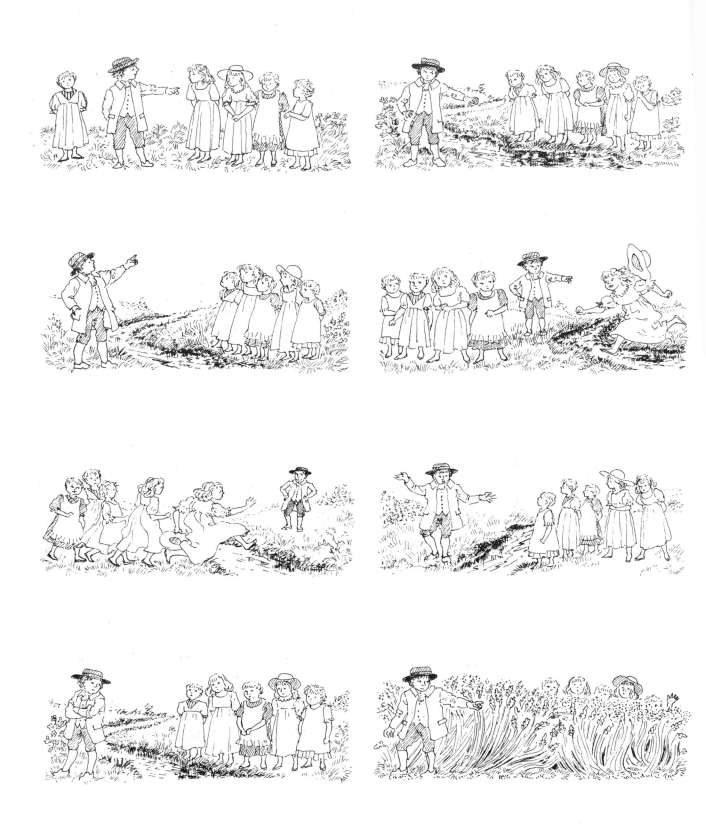